THE DANCING
PALM TREE

THE DANCING PALM TREE

AND OTHER NIGERIAN FOLKTALES

RETOLD BY BARBARA K. WALKER
WOODCUTS BY HELEN SIEGL

TEXAS TECH UNIVERSITY PRESS
1990

Credits

To *The Instructor* for "A Lesson for the Bat" (appeared as "Why the Bat Is Ashamed to Be Seen" in the issue of October 1965). Used by permission.

To *Humpty Dumpty's Magazine for Little Children* for "It's All the Fault of Adam" (appeared as "Adam and the Woodcutter" in the issue of December 1965). Used by permission.

To The Shoe String Press for permission to adapt "The Hunter and the Deer," which appeared originally in *Nigerian Folk Tales*, edited by Barbara K. and Warren S. Walker, second edition (The Shoe String Press, Archon Books, 1980).

Text Copyright © 1968, 1990 Barbara Walker
Illustrations Copyright © 1990 Helen Siegl

Printed in the United States of America.
This book was set in 13 on 17 Weiss and printed on acid-free paper that meets the guidelines for permanence and durability of the Committee on Production Guidelines for Book Longevity of the Council on Library Resources. ♾
Original book design by Mildred Phillips (Kantrowitz); adaptations for this edition by Cameron Poulter

Library of Congress Cataloging-in-Publication Data

Walker, Barbara K.
  The dancing palm tree and other Nigerian folktales / retold by
Barbara K. Walker ; woodcuts by Helen Siegl.
    p.   cm.
  Reprint. Originally published: New York : Parents' Magazine Press,
1968.
  Summary: This collection of eleven tales from Nigeria includes
"The Boy and the Leopard," "The King and the Ring," and "The Reward
of Treachery." Also contains a glossary and explanation of customs.
  ISBN 0-89672-216-3 (alk. paper)
  1. Tales—Nigeria. [1. Folklore—Nigeria.] I. Siegl, Helen,
ill. II. Title.
PZ8.1.W128Dan   1990
398.2'09669—dc20   89-27748
                                                    CIP
Texas Tech University Press   AC
Lubbock, Texas 79409-1037 USA   91-684

Manufactured in Japan by Dai Nippon Co., Ltd.

**"Printed in the United States of America"
should read "Printed in Japan."**

For Dr. Olawale Idewu,
whose love of his country and of its treasury of folk tales
led to the making of this book.

CONTENTS

THE DANCING
PALM TREE

INTRODUCTION

The Dancing Palm Tree and Other Nigerian Folktales offers to children everywhere a little taste of the literary heritage shared every day by their counterparts in Nigeria. Village or hamlet, town or city, any locality where people can gather finds an eager circle of listeners ready to hear the tales that have come down from family to family there in West Africa for hundreds of years. And the old tales are just as entertaining and as instructive and as appealing today as they were when they were first told.

All the tales in this collection were told by Olawale Idewu, a young Nigerian student in an American college, lonesome for home and happy to share the stories that are part of his heritage. Ola's homeland is Western Nigeria, populated largely by a people known as the Yorubas, a proud, ambitious, sociable people that have long been among the leaders in Nigeria. And the influence of the Yorubas and other peoples of West Africa has spread farther than one might suspect, for most Afro-Americans who now live in the United States and in Latin America can trace their origins to exactly that part of Africa. Here, then, can be found some of the tales which are a rightful part of the heritage of a tenth of our own population, and thus a part of the heritage of us all.

Suppose yourself for a moment in Western Nigeria on a moonlit evening. The day's work has been done, and friends and neighbors have gathered together to talk. Suddenly one among the group turns to an older man sitting at the edge of the piazza. "Tell us a story," he begs. And he knows what he is asking, for many in the group can tell stories, and very well indeed. Before the story is begun, there is a pause for the asking of riddles, a traditional preparation for story-telling.

Q. What dares to knock a king on the head?

A. A knife, because even a king must shave.

Q. What is it that goes past the palace and does not stop to greet the king?

A. The stream, for it flows past the palace speaking to no one at all.

Q. What god requires a sacrifice of every man, woman, and child at least twice a day?

A. The throat, for it will have its food.

The audience, by puzzling out the answers, opens its ears to learn what the story has to tell.

The story is then begun, and it is as much a play and a musical performance as a story, because the storyteller really becomes a part of the story, imitating sounds and gestures, acting out what happens, singing the songs the characters sing, prostrating himself where some unfortunate fellow in the tale must humble himself before a superior. Many of the listeners take part, too, in the telling, joining in on the songs, beating drums and playing other instruments to increase the effect of the story. And if the story has been especially good, there will be cheering and clapping for the storyteller at the end.

No man under twenty-one is allowed to tell stories in such a gathering, but all through childhood boys and girls tell stories among their friends, preparing for the day when they will be asked to tell a story on just such a moonlit evening to please or entertain or instruct their friends and neighbors.

Many of the stories begin, "Far away and long ago in a small village," for this is a tradition in Yoruba storytelling. And somewhere in each story there is likely to be a "moral," a human truth which is taught through what happens in the story. For one of the main purposes of storytelling in Nigeria has always been to teach, to instruct, a very important function in a land where until just recently there were few schools and where many of the important lessons of life were learned at the knee of the storyteller. But you will find that the truths taught in these stories prevail not only in Nigeria but all around the world, truths that people must learn to live by no matter what country they call home. In their Nigerian dress, these truths will seem new and fresh and interesting. And through these tales, it is hoped, we shall all become better acquainted with our brothers in West Africa.

Barbara K. Walker
Lubbock, Texas

THE DANCING PALM TREE

LONG AGO AND FAR AWAY in a little village there were two good friends, a tortoise and a farmer. Most of the people in this village earned their food by farming, raising yams and corn and cassava and beans. But this farmer counted himself especially blessed in having the tortoise as his friend. For although the tortoise was too slow and clumsy to help with the hoeing and harvesting, he had a very powerful sense of smell, and he could follow the tracks of bush rats and rabbits to their holes. Then the farmer would set traps for these small animals, and the two were thus able to add meat to their table.

Unfortunately, one day the farmer died very suddenly, and Tortoise was left to fend for himself. Tortoise did not know how to farm; he could not even set traps to catch the small animals whose tracks he found. Since Tortoise was a very clever fellow, and since he found eating necessary to his comfort, he began to think very hard about how he might gain his daily food without too much effort.

As he sat thinking, the people of the village began going past with their baskets full of produce—corn and yams and cassava and beans.

They were taking these and other good things to the marketplace in the town not far away through the forest. Men trudged by with loads of firewood and other articles to trade at the market.

"Hmn," thought Tortoise. "Every four days the marketplace is filled with food and goods of all kinds. People are chatting, meeting old friends and trading bits of news along with their farm produce. Such a place should have something good for a hungry tortoise. But how is this affair to be managed?"

At last he had figured out a fine plan. When everyone had gone by to market, Tortoise crawled to a certain palm tree a hundred yards or so from the open market. Clumsily he wedged himself into a hole near the foot of the tree. Safe inside, he began to sing:

> *Palm tree, dance.*
> *Dance all around the marketplace.*
> *Dance all around the marketplace.*

Now, Tortoise was a wise creature, with certain special powers of magic. As soon as the palm tree heard this song, it picked up its roots and began to whirl down the forest path toward the market.

Imagine the surprise of the farmers and their wives when they saw a palm tree dancing toward them! At first they stood amazed. "What is this? A dancing palm tree? This has never happened before!" They waited curiously to see what would happen. And every minute the palm tree danced closer to the marketplace, and the people still stood watching.

"This is something strange. I'm going to get out of here!" one man exclaimed, and he began to run. Then everyone began to run here and there—mothers looking for their crying children, and wives looking for their husbands. In a very short time the marketplace was emptied of people. But in their haste they had left behind corn, yams, cassava, palm oil, and all kinds of good things. When the marketplace was entirely quiet, Tortoise directed the palm tree to stop dancing. He looked around here and there to be sure that everybody was gone. Then he crawled out very slowly and went around the market gathering up the things he liked and storing them in the palm tree. When he was quite satisfied with what he had collected, he wedged himself back into the hole near the foot of the palm tree, and the palm tree danced back to the place it had come from. Tortoise waited until dark and then crawled home with his booty.

Meanwhile, the people had gathered together and had sent delegates to the *oba*, the king of the chief village.

"Your Highness," the delegates began, "something unusual happened in the market today. We have never seen such a thing in our lives before, and we could scarcely believe it. Will you please help us?"

"Well? What happened?"

"Sire, a palm tree was dancing."

The king laughed. "You must have been drinking too much palm wine! A dancing palm tree! Have you ever heard of anything as ridiculous as that?"

"Believe us, sire, we had never heard of anything like it. It surprised us so that we could scarcely trust our eyes. But it did happen."

"You don't know what you are talking about," the king said, drawing his robe about him and rising. "Go back. I have much better things to do than to listen to a tale like this."

The delegates went back to the people at the market. "The king did not believe us," they reported. "He was certain we were telling him lies."

The people grumbled among themselves for a little while, and then one old man said, "Well, this has never happened before. Perhaps it will not happen again." And they gathered up what was left of their produce and went home.

But early in the morning of the next market day, Tortoise discovered that his food supply was very low. "That I ate and was satisfied yesterday does not serve to meet my hunger today," said he. "I must go again to the market." And well before the farmers and their wives had started along the footpath, Tortoise crawled to the same palm tree and wedged himself inside it, waiting for the moment when the marketplace would be filled with people and goods.

> *Palm tree, dance.*
> *Dance all around the marketplace.*
> *Dance all around the marketplace,*

he sang. And the palm tree picked up its roots and began to whirl down the forest path toward the marketplace.

Again the people were astounded to see a palm tree dancing to market. And again they fled, leaving their goods behind them.

Tortoise stayed inside the palm tree until everyone had gone, and then quietly he crawled from his hole in the tree and went to make his choice among the things in the market. He took nothing that was cheap or of poor quality. Only the finest produce was carried back to be stored in the palm tree. Quite satisfied, he wedged himself into his hole near the foot of the palm tree, and the tree danced back to its place in the forest.

Once more the people sent delegates to the king urging him to look into the matter. This business of the dancing palm tree was no lie; the king must surely take it seriously this time. But when the king had heard their story, he said, "This cannot be true. Have you lost your wits entirely? A dancing palm tree! We shall see about that."

On the next market day the king sent three of his messengers. All morning they watched, but nothing happened. Just as one of the messengers was grumbling about the nonsensical tale told by the delegates, the dancing palm tree came whirling down the forest path toward the marketplace.

"See! There it comes," called one of the messengers. And they looked and looked as the palm tree danced toward them. The people who had seen the palm tree dance on other market days ran wildly one way and another. But the king's messengers said, "Let us wait a bit longer and see what happens." Closer and closer the palm tree came, and one by one the messengers took to their heels.

They wasted no time in getting to the king. "It is true!" they gasped. "We ourselves have seen the dancing palm tree."

"Have you become mad?" exclaimed the king. "Do you really think you have seen a dancing palm tree?"

"Surely we saw it. And if you saw it, you would believe it, too."

"No, I would never believe it, for it is not so," the king insisted.

"Sire, please come and see for yourself."

"I come, myself? Indeed not! I have no time for such foolishness. But I shall send my chief adviser. *He* will not be deceived by nonsense."

Before the next market day, Tortoise had finished all his food, so as usual he went to the palm tree very early in the morning and crawled inside. Late in the morning, when trading in the market had reached its height, Tortoise sang,

> *Palm tree, dance.*
> *Dance all around the marketplace.*
> *Dance all around the marketplace.*

And the palm tree went dancing on its way.

The people marketing were the first to run away, then the messengers who had seen the palm tree dance before. But the chief adviser was a very dignified man. "I shall not run," he told himself, "until it is absolutely necessary. After all, I have been sent by the king to defend the people." He waited as the palm tree danced closer, and closer, and closer. Finally his teeth began to clack with fear. "I cannot stand this any longer," said he, and he took to his heels and ran all the way back to the palace.

When he came before the king, he was so short of breath he could not speak at all for the first three minutes.

"What is wrong?" the king demanded. "Tell me what is wrong!"

"Huh-uh-huh-uh-huh," puffed the king's adviser. "Sire, I must catch my breath." But finally he said, "It was a strange thing, your Highness. I saw a dancing palm tree."

"What! *You* saw it? Then I must see it myself. This is a serious matter." The following market day, the king called all his household together and they went with great ceremony to the marketplace.

As for Tortoise, he had begun to realize that his good fortune must soon come to an end. "After all," he remembered, "the god who favors a lazy man does not exist. On the other hand," he reasoned, "there is no god like the throat; it demands sacrifices daily." But though he hid himself inside the palm tree, he waited a long time before commanding it to dance.

When the time came and went and the dancing palm tree did not appear, the delegates and the messengers and the king's adviser trembled, fearful that the tree would not appear at all, and that the king would account them liars. Just before high noon, however, the dancing palm tree whirled into the marketplace. The people doing their marketing ran away; the messengers ran away; the king's adviser ran away; all the guards for the king ran away. But the king himself was very brave. It was unthinkable for a king to run. He stood still as the dancing palm tree moved closer, and closer, and closer, trying his best to hold on to his courage. Nevertheless, when the palm tree was very, very close he just could not stay there any longer. Truly, he had never seen anything like this in his life before, so he ran. He lost his crown and his shoes and his scepter, and he arrived at the palace wearing only a single robe.

Everyone in the village marveled to see the king running like a thief. "There must be something very bad about this dancing palm tree," they agreed.

The next morning, the king sent his messengers through the surrounding villages to call all the wisest men and the magicians to assemble at his palace. When they met, the king told them all that had happened. "And," he concluded, "to the man among you who is able to solve this problem I shall give half of all I possess."

Now, all the wise men had heard about the dancing palm tree and had wondered about it, but there was only one of them—an old man with much experience—who was willing to undertake the task. "Sire, I shall do it," he offered. As for the king, he was scarcely able to believe his ears, he was so certain that nothing could be done to stop the palm tree from dancing.

The old man set to work and made Sigidi, a seated image of a man, from clay. It looked so real that everyone who saw it fully expected it to move and speak. Then the wise man painted Sigidi with *amo*, a sticky substance. When the time came for market day, he arose very early and took the image to the very center of the marketplace; he left Sigidi there and hid himself near the top of a tall tree where he could see everything that happened.

As for Tortoise, his food supply had dwindled to little but yam skins. "I must get myself something to eat," he decided. As usual, he crawled to the palm tree early in the morning and wedged himself inside. When the marketing had reached its height he sang,

> *Palm tree, dance.*
> *Dance all around the marketplace.*
> *Dance all around the marketplace.*

And the palm tree picked up its roots and whirled down the forest path toward the market. And, as usual, everyone in the marketplace fled.

Or *had* everyone left? To Tortoise's surprise, a man still remained, sitting calmly at the very center of the marketplace.

"How can this be?" wondered Tortoise. But as the palm tree danced closer and closer, Tortoise remembered. "Of course! There are always one or two who stay until the last minute, and they run afterwards."

As the palm tree danced closer, the man still sat there.

"What!" Tortoise was surprised, and he watched the man through the hole in the palm tree. "He is just holding on to his courage a little longer than the rest," Tortoise decided.

Closer and closer and closer the palm tree danced, and still the man did not move. Tortoise hesitated for some time. "Shall I go out? Shall I stay inside? Or shall I dance back to the forest?" But a hungry person has no mind for anything other than food. "I shall go out," Tortoise said. "Perhaps when I talk to him he will run away."

Tortoise crawled out of the palm tree and went boldly over to the man. "Look here," he said. "Who do you think you are?"

The man said nothing.

"Can you hear me? I am talking to *you*. What do you think you are, sitting here when all the others have run away?"

Still the man did not answer.

"You must answer me. If you do not, I shall give you a hard slap."

There was still no answer from the man.

Whap! Tortoise gave the man a hard slap on the right cheek. And Tortoise's hand stuck fast to Sigidi.

"You! What do you think you are doing? Let me loose! Let me loose, or I shall use my left hand and give you a harder slap."

Sigidi still did not say anything, and *Whup!* Tortoise gave the man a hard slap with his left hand. His left hand also became stuck.

"Now, listen to me," said Tortoise. "This has gone far enough. Let my hands loose. I am talking to *you*!"

Still the man said nothing.

"Since my hands are not free, I shall give you a kick with my right foot!" exclaimed Tortoise angrily. *Whap!* And his right foot stuck fast.

Whup! He kicked with his left foot, and his left foot stuck fast. "This is serious," thought Tortoise in despair. "How am I ever to get away from this man?

"Please let me go," he begged. "I am sorry I spoke to you like that, but *please* let me go."

Suddenly the wise old man came down from the tree where he had been hiding. "Aha, Tortoise! *You* are the one that has been troubling us. Now I have caught you." He pulled Tortoise loose from the sticky image and took him to the king.

The king was greatly surprised. "Tortoise! *You*, of all creatures! You

little crawly thing! Do you know you have turned the whole village into tumult? And you made me run, short of breath, to the palace, like a thief in my own kingdom! Well you know that no one should expect to live by the sweat of others' brows. We are not going to spare you. You shall suffer punishment worthy of such deceit."

Tortoise was put into a guarded room, and on the following day the king sent his messengers to tell all the villagers that his wise man had caught the troublemaker, and that they should come to see who had been responsible for the dancing palm tree. When the villagers came, they could scarcely believe that Tortoise had been the cause of their alarm.

After everyone had seen Tortoise, the king ordered his chief adviser to run a sword through the troublemaker, and he was relieved forever both of his hunger and of his power to trick.

But since Tortoise had not sent the palm tree back to its place in the forest, it took root in the center of the marketplace. And beneath it the children still sit on market days to hear the story of Tortoise and the dancing palm tree.

THE HUNTER AND THE HIND

FAR AWAY AND LONG AGO in a little village there lived a young man who was gentle by birth but a hunter by necessity. He was the handsomest man in the village, and he was known as a fine hunter because he had never come home from a hunt empty-handed.

One day this young man went out into the forest to hunt. As was his custom, he climbed a certain tree to watch for prey worthy of his skill. But this day, though he watched long and patiently, no prey appeared. At sunset, as he was preparing to leave for home, he saw a hind coming toward him through the forest. Eagerly he fitted an arrow to the string of his bow, ready to shoot. To his surprise, the hind paused near the tree and began to remove its skin. In his amazement, he forgot to shoot, but sat quietly watching the hind.

Before his eyes, the hind became a beautiful woman. Carefully she

17

hid the hind skin beneath a stone near the tree and walked gracefully through the forest toward the next village. After she had disappeared, the hunter returned his arrow to his quiver and climbed down. Going to the stone where the woman had hidden the hind skin, he removed the skin and looked at it. It was much the same as any other hind skin. Nonetheless, he chose to put it into his game bag. Then he went home. But he said nothing at all to his wife about the matter.

Early the next morning he arose and returned to his place in the same tree in the forest, determined to watch for the return of the beautiful woman as well as for suitable prey. The day passed without a sign of any animal except a large snake, which slithered away before he could capture it. The sun was just touching the rim of the horizon when the beautiful woman came walking quietly through the forest. Silently the hunter watched her as she went to the stone and lifted it up to recover her skin. She wept to find it gone, and beat her breast and tore her hair in her grief. Not finding the skin where she had left it, she hurried from stone to bush to tree, as if it must surely be found somewhere nearby.

At last the hunter spoke. "What are you looking for?"

Without raising her eyes, the woman replied, "I left something here yesterday, and I must find it before nightfall."

"What will you give me if I find it for you?" he asked.

But the woman gave no answer. She searched even more feverishly for the skin, scratching her arms and bruising her hands in her search among the rocks and bushes.

"I think perhaps I could help you find the hind skin," said the hunter.

At the mention of the skin, the woman looked up and saw the

hunter seated in the tree. "Ah, if you could get me the hind skin, I should give you anything you wish," she said gratefully.

"Then," said the hunter, "I shall give you the skin if you will promise to be my wife."

The woman smiled. "You know I cannot be your wife. Now please give me my skin, if you have found it."

"Well," the hunter replied, "if you are not willing to give me what I ask, then I shall keep the skin."

At last the woman agreed to become the hunter's wife. "But," said she, "not everything seen by the eye should be spoken by the mouth. You must promise to tell no human being what you have seen."

The hunter promised never to reveal her secret. Then he came down from the tree, and the two went through the forest to his village. Since the woman had no wish now to become a hind again, she did not ask for the skin, and the hunter kept it in his game bag.

On entering the village, they were met by many neighbors curious about the beautiful woman. In answer to their questions, the hunter replied only that he had met her in another town. But to his first wife he told a fuller story: he had met the woman in a nearby town, and since she had no living relatives, the king of that town had insisted that he take her as his bride. When a king insists, what can one do but obey?

Well, the first wife was distressed. After all, she had no wish for another woman in the household. And the new wife was very beautiful. But she accepted the woman without protest. Other men in the village had two wives, and she must make the best she could of the matter.

But from time to time this new wife behaved rather strangely. Sometimes she lapped her soup from the plate, instead of using a spoon. Often she sat in a corner on the floor, instead of joining the hunter and his senior wife at the table. Occasionally she would eat no meals with them at all, but would content herself with scraping the bits of food from the cauldrons after the others had gone to bed. The senior wife was very curious about these things, and she asked her husband again and again about the woman, but he refused to tell her anything beyond the tale he had told her that first evening. "I have already told you all I can," he insisted. "I love you. How can you expect more than that?"

But the senior wife was not satisfied, and at last in her distress she told one of her friends about the strange behavior of this new woman. "How can I learn more about her?" she asked. "I must know."

Taking a special powder from her shelf, the friend gave it to the senior wife. "Prepare a good dinner for your husband tomorrow," said she. "Serve him plenty of palm wine, and to the third calabash of palm wine add this powder. It will loosen his tongue, and he will tell you what you want to know."

The next evening the senior wife served her husband an especially good meal, and into the third calabash of palm wine she slipped the powder. Then, since the new wife had gone some distance to the village well to draw fresh water, the senior wife approached the hunter. "My beloved husband," she began, "can't you tell me more about this beautiful woman? I am interested."

Lulled by the fine dinner and the drugged wine, the hunter told his first wife the whole story. "I have kept the skin hidden there on my

attic shelf because I know not what will happen to me or to her if it is destroyed," he concluded. "I look at it now and then, but I have not returned it to her."

The wife listened to the tale, but said nothing. And at length the hunter slept.

The following morning after the hunter had left, the senior wife began to prepare a soup for the evening meal. As usual, she called the new wife to help her, but this time the new wife accidentally added sugar instead of salt to the soup.

The senior wife said crossly, "Look, my good woman. No matter how long you have been with us, you scarcely behave as a human being!"

"What do you mean?" asked the second wife, puzzled.

"If you are to live with human beings you must behave as a human being. Your behavior is more like that of an animal. And if you cannot show respect for me, at least show politeness!"

Angered, the new wife ran to the first wife and struck her across the face. Instead of returning the blow, the senior wife hurried to the attic shelf where her husband kept the hind skin. She flung the skin into the face of the new wife. "There is your skin!" she shouted. "I shall be happy to have you gone from this house."

Beside herself with rage, the new wife slipped into the hind skin. With her sharp, hard hoofs she killed the senior wife. Then she left the hut and went off into the forest as a hind. She ran until she found the hunter, seated in the same tree where he had been when she first saw him. As the hunter was fitting an arrow to his bowstring, the hind spoke. "Oh, my beloved, do not shoot at me. I trusted you, but you have betrayed my trust. Go home now to what is left to you.

Remember, I loved you, but you have forfeited that love." And the hind ran off into the forest.

The hunter was speechless with wonder. Putting his arrow into his quiver, he descended the tree and hurried toward his village. But the news had taken wing, and the villagers were gathered before his hut, silent and sad. Going inside, he found the body of his first wife. And the hind skin was gone from the shelf. His head bowed in grief, he went outside again, to be told the story of the quarrel between the two women and its bitter ending.

Well he understood the feeling of the villagers. Once deceived, they would never believe him again. Life turned to ashes for him, and at length he died, lonely and uncared for. Thus it is when one does evil to others: most of all, he injures himself.

ASHOREMASHIKA

LONG AGO AND FAR AWAY near a small village there lived a kindhearted farmer. His farm and his hut were right next to the footpath between his village and the big market town where the *oba* (king) lived.

Because of his generosity and his love for his neighbors, this farmer kept a basket of tasty foods hanging on the post in front of his hut. As his friends and neighbors passed by, they were invited to take from the basket whatever they wanted of the foods they found there— baked yams or baked corn, perhaps, or fresh fruit. And the farmer was well loved in turn by all the people in that part of the countryside, for all at one time or another had feasted from his basket.

As they passed his farm, they would call out in greeting, giving him the name Ashoremashika, which means "The Man Who Always Does Good and Never Does Evil." In answer to their greeting, Ashoremashika would look up from hoeing his yams or tending his beans. "There is something in the basket for you!" he would call. "Please reach in and help yourself."

At length, however, a mean-minded man in the village became jealous of Ashoremashika's popularity. One day this man determined to cause such grave trouble for Ashoremashika that none of the villagers would like him or seek out his company. Indeed, the villagers would come to hate his very name.

Capturing a poisonous snake, this man hid it in a bag and began to walk along the footpath toward Ashoremashika's hut. As was the custom, he called out a greeting to Ashoremashika, and the kind farmer answered cheerfully, "There is some food in the basket for you, neighbor. Please reach in and help yourself."

Taking advantage of his opportunity, the man dropped the poisonous snake into the basket on the pretense of reaching in for something good to eat. Then he walked slowly along the footpath toward the market town. A few rods farther along the path he met the village bellman, coming with a message from the king. The two greeted each other, and then the bellman went on toward the village. Eager to see what would happen, the mean-minded man stepped aside into some bushes for a moment or two and then walked quietly back toward Ashoremashika's farm. Yes, he heard the bellman greet Ashoremashika, and he heard Ashoremashika invite the bellman to help himself to whatever was in the basket. In a moment there was a pained cry from the bellman, and both Ashoremashika and the mean-minded villager ran toward the sound.

On the ground near the post slumped the bellman, clutching his wrist and moaning in anguish. And Ashoremashika came up just in time to see the snake slither off into the brush.

"Oh, my dear Ashoremashika," said the villager reproachfully. "Why did you do it?"

"Do *what?*" asked the puzzled farmer, staring at the man.

"Why did you put a snake in your basket? We all trusted you. How can we ever trust you again?" And the villager seemed truly sorrowful.

The more Ashoremashika protested his innocence, the more the villager reproached him. And Ashoremashika, knowing full well the danger of his position, sighed in despair.

The two carried the bellman to his home in the village, and the doctors and magicians were called. But despite their efforts, the bell-man died of the snake's bite.

As for Ashoremashika, what could he do? No matter how much the villagers wanted to believe in his innocence, there was still the evidence of the crime: the bellman had been invited by Ashoremashika to put his hand into the basket, and had immediately been bitten by the snake. Who but Ashoremashika would put anything *into* the basket? And if witnesses were needed, there were two: the dead bellman, with the marks of the snake's fangs in his wrist, and the man from the village who had been near Ashoremashika's house when the bellman was bitten. Shortly Ashoremashika was thrown into prison for his crime.

As chance would have it, the king's youngest daughter was to be married the following week, and in the midst of preparations for the wedding the king neglected to order Ashoremashika's execution. The evening before the wedding, Ashoremashika was sitting alone in his cell when there came a strange *hshsh!* sound along the corridor, and into Ashoremashika's cell slithered the same snake which had bitten the bellman. Coming close to Ashoremashika, it spat out a small packet at his feet. Then it hissed a message which stirred hope in the farmer's heart.

The snake, knowing full well that the villager, not Ashoremashika, was guilty of the bellman's death, planned to win Ashoremashika's release from prison by a curious means: He would bite the king's youngest daughter that night, on the eve of her wedding day, and she would appear to die. Ashoremashika would offer to bring back the life of the princess in return for his own release from prison. The snake told the farmer that the powder in the packet he had brought would surely heal the princess if it could be dissolved in the blood of a murderer and the resulting potion be applied to the snakebite. As for a murderer, he could depend upon the evil-minded villager who had brought blame upon Ashoremashika for the death of the bellman, but who was in truth guilty of the death himself.

Ashoremashika gratefully accepted the plan offered by the snake, and the snake left the cell. A short time afterwards, there was a great weeping and wailing in the streets of the market town. In the midst of the merrymaking, the king's youngest daughter had been bitten by a deadly snake, and she had been carried fainting to her bed.

The next morning a steady procession of doctors and magicians tried all the potions and spells at their command, but no remedy could bring the princess back to life. Sadly the king called a halt to the wedding preparations and arranged instead for his daughter's funeral.

Meanwhile, Ashoremashika had been visited by several of his friends, and to each of them in turn the farmer had said he could bring the princess back to life if he were permitted to try his special medicine. His words took wing and came quickly to the ear of the king. Ashoremashika was bidden to appear before the king and make good the claim he had made. For his part, the king promised that the princess's cure would bring Ashoremashika's release from prison. Learning that the potion required the blood of a murderer, the king ordered that blood be drawn from the farmer, since he had been imprisoned for murder of the bellman. Half the packet of magical powder was added to a small calabash of Ashoremashika's blood and the medicine was applied to the wound. The princess stirred not at all.

"Aha!" exclaimed the king. "Your claim was false, was it not?"

"Sire," said Ashoremashika, "I am not a murderer. Let us seek the blood of a murderer—that village man who was at hand when the bellman died."

The king, anxious above all for the recovery of his daughter, sent

for the evil-minded villager, and required of him blood for the princess's cure. The blood was drawn. Dissolving the rest of the powder in the villager's blood, Ashoremashika applied the medicine to the snakebite on the princess's wrist. Within a moment the princess sighed, stretched, and wondered to find herself in bed.

The villager, knowing not at all why he had been chosen to furnish blood for the miraculous cure, found himself accused of the crime which he had indeed committed, revealed only through the magic healing. In due course, he made a full confession and met his death as a murderer.

As for Ashoremashika, he was released from prison and restored to his old life in the hut along the footpath.

THE KING AND THE RING

FAR AWAY AND LONG AGO in a little town there lived a king who was a very powerful ruler. In the same town there lived a man who called himself No-King-Is-as-Great-as-God. One day the king heard about this man, and he was greatly annoyed. Surely a man bearing such a name was a threat to the dignity of the king. But how was he to be punished? After all, he had merely stated in his name what he believed; he had done no wrong.

Nevertheless, the king resolved to bring such great harm to No-King-Is-as-Great-as-God that his name would thereafter be mocked instead of honored. Only then could the king feel comfortable and respected in his kingdom. Accordingly, the king sent his chief adviser to bring No-King-Is-as-Great-as-God to the palace, and the man was brought within the hour.

"Tell me," the king began. "What is your name?"

"My name, sire, is No-King-Is-as-Great-as-God."

"And you believe, do you, that God is greater than any king?"

"Yes, sire, I do."

"Hmph!" said the king. "You may be right. We shall see. Meanwhile, for your courage and honesty let me give you this gold ring. It bears the sign of the royal family. Guard it well, for it is a mark of our friendship."

"Indeed I shall, sire!" exclaimed the man, placing the ring carefully in an inside pocket. All the way home he kept patting his pocket to make certain that the ring was still there.

But when the man's wife saw the ring, she was very uneasy about it. "This may be a trick to find you faithless in some matter or another. Suppose you should lose the ring? Would he not accuse you of considering his friendship of little worth? Come, my dear. Let us find a safe hiding place for it somewhere about our house. Then we can feel at ease about it."

After weighing the matter in his mind, the man agreed with his wife that it would be wise to hide the ring where only they could find it. Accordingly, that evening they dug a small hole in the inside wall of their hut and buried the ring there, smoothing the hiding place afterwards and hanging a rush mat over it so that they could surely find it again.

From time to time the king sent for No-King-Is-as-Great-as-God, to talk with him or to entertain him at a dinner, pretending all the while to a great and growing friendship for him. These visits served only to make No-King-Is-as-Great-as-God more and more suspicious of the king. "What can he want of me, do you suppose?" he asked his wife as he was about to leave for the palace for his third dinner there.

"My dear, I have no notion. But he surely means you no good," his wife replied. "He has a plan of some sort, you may be certain."

"Yes, my wife. And we must try to please him in every way we can."

One day while the woman was at home alone, a messenger came from the king. "The king wishes to see you this morning. Come with me," said he, and she followed him out of the hut and through the town to the palace.

The king appeared very friendly. He smiled as he greeted her, and motioned her to be seated. Then, "I should like to prepare a little surprise for your husband," said he. "He and I have become such good friends that I have decided we shall wear rings to match. Do you suppose that you could slip the ring away from him and bring it to me so that I could have a ring made for myself which matches it exactly? I have forgotten just how the design is arranged."

The woman thought for a moment. She and her husband had agreed not to touch the ring until the king sent for it. Should she take it out, or wait for her husband to take it to the king?

When the woman hesitated to answer, the king spoke again. "I have just the right position in mind for your husband, and I wish to give suitable honor to you both. Surely you wish to please me, too?"

Then the woman remembered what her husband had said: "We must try to please him in every way we can." She smiled at the king. "Surely. I shall get the ring for you."

"Fine," said the king. "I shall send my chief adviser this afternoon to get it from you."

The woman hurried through the winding streets to her hut. Carefully she removed the rush mat and dug here and there in the wall until she had found the ring. Just as she had replaced the mat, the king's chief adviser came to secure the ring. Holding it firmly in his hand, he left, to go directly to the palace. As for the woman, she decided to say nothing at all to her husband about the ring.

Several days later, the king sent for No-King-Is-as-Great-as-God. When he had arrived at the palace, the king said to him, "Come, now. Let me see how my ring looks on your hand. I have not seen it since I gave it to you many weeks ago."

"Ah, sire," replied the man, "I value it too much to wear it every day. I have no wish to lose it, so I have hidden it in a safe place."

The king scowled. "Is that how much you value our friendship? I do not hesitate to invite you to the palace, and to make much over you. Are you ashamed of our friendship, that you do not wear the ring? A ring such as that is meant to be worn, not hidden away from all eyes."

"I shall wear it if you wish, sire," said the man. "It is in truth a beautiful ring, and I shall be proud to wear it before all men."

"I do not believe you," the king declared. "I am certain that you no longer have the ring, or you would be wearing it as a mark of our friendship. You must have sold it, or lost it, or given it away. And I suspect that you will not be able to produce it even if you are given the space of seven days to do so. I shall be fair, however. Since you are certain you have the ring, if you come before me seven days hence bearing the ring, you may ask whatever you wish of me, even if it be my *life*, and it shall be granted. If, on the other hand, you do *not* produce the ring, I shall be free to demand of you anything I choose, since you will have failed to honor our friendship. You may be sure the punishment will be severe."

"Be it as you say, sire," answered the man, confident that he would be able to wear the ring on the required day. And the king, too, was well satisfied with the agreement, since he already had the ring in his possession. But as soon as he had dismissed No-King-Is-as-Great-as-God, the king walked straight to the edge of the sea and threw the ring as far as he could throw it into the rolling waters. "There!" he exclaimed. "Now no one will be able to steal the ring from me, and No-King-Is-as-Great-as-God will reap the punishment that he deserves for the boldness of his name."

As for No-King-Is-as-Great-as-God, leaving the presence of the king, he hurried home to tell his wife that it was just as they had suspected: the king had used the ring as a trap. But when he had told his wife, she could only shake her head and weep. "It is too late!" she cried. And she told her husband of her own summons by the king a few days earlier, and of her surrender of the ring to the king's chief adviser.

In truth, there was now little hope for No-King-Is-as-Great-as-God. How could he produce the ring if the king already had it? In the midst of their grieving, however, the wife remembered something. "Tell me," said she. "What is your name?"

"Why, you know my name!" exclaimed the husband in surprise. "It is No-King-Is-as-Great-as-God."

"Do you believe what your name says?" she asked.

"Of *course* I do," he answered.

"Then let us not grieve," said his wife. "If it is God's will, you will be spared. After all, it is the Lord who decides whether or not we prosper. One man beats the drum for the downfall of another, but God the King determines whether or not the drum will sound. Let us trust in God."

"You are right, my wife. And whatever may happen seven days hence, we must not waste these hours together in grieving. Come, let us plan a feast for our friends and neighbors for the morrow," suggested the man. And they agreed that they would purchase several of the finest fish in the market, as a special delicacy.

The next day while the two were cutting open the fresh fish, No-King-Is-as-Great-as-God suddenly cried out, "Look, my wife! Look!"

She hurried to his side and there, just released from the belly of the largest fish, was the gold ring. In relief and joy the two laughed and wept together. Then, after carefully washing the ring, they returned it for safekeeping to the hole in the wall of their house, covering it again with the rush mat.

There was rejoicing and singing and drumming and dancing in the home of No-King-Is-as-Great-as-God the entire week. The king, hearing of the celebration, marveled at the madness of a man who could sing in the face of certain death. But his marveling turned to wrath when No-King-Is-as-Great-as-God sent a message to the palace reading, "O king, there is truly no king as great as God!" Surely the man must die for his rash behavior.

The seventh day came, and the king, the better to savor his victory, summoned all the townspeople to assemble before the palace for a meeting. Just before the appointed hour, No-King-Is-as-Great-as-God went with his wife on horseback, with drummers before them and with dancing, straight to the front of the palace. Indeed this seemed a strange man, to go with drums and dancing to his own execution!

There in front of the gathering the king announced the terms of his agreement with No-King-Is-as-Great-as-God, including the punishment to be awarded the man should he fail to produce the ring.

"And, sire, have you forgotten what was to follow if I *should* produce the ring?" asked No-King-Is-as-Great-as-God.

"I have not," the king responded, and he laughed as he spoke. "If— *if*—this man should produce the ring—which he *cannot*—then he may demand whatever he wishes of me—yes, even my *life*, if he so choose. But we shall see . . . Now, No-King-Is-as-Great-as-God, produce the ring, if you can."

Quietly No-King-Is-as-Great-as-God reached into the pocket of his robe and drawing forth the ring he slipped it upon his own finger. A roar of wonder and approval swept the crowd. As for the king, consternation sat upon his face. There was no question about it: the ring was there, bright in the sunlight. Only the hand of God could have altered this contest.

It remained now but for No-King-Is-as-Great-as-God to ask what he would of the king. In keeping with custom, he required that the king die. And shortly afterwards No-King-Is-as-Great-as-God was himself made king of the town.

A SECRET TOLD TO A STRANGER

AR AWAY AND LONG AGO in a little village there lived a hunter who was famous among his people for skill in hunting. Besides being brave and skillful and clever, this hunter had certain magical powers. Many were the tales told of his miraculous escapes from maddened elephants and snarling tigers and awesome crocodiles.

At last, word had come to the animals in the bush country that this hunter's magical powers enabled him to change his shape from that of a man to that of living forms of various kinds. Thus, just at the moment he was about to be destroyed by some fierce animal, he would disappear, and only a crashing through the brush or the swaying of a leaf would show where he had gone in his new form. Since the elephants had suffered the greatest loss from the hunter's skill, it was agreed by the animals that an elephant should attempt to learn the hunter's secret so that he might be destroyed and the animals might dwell thereafter free from terror.

Now it chanced that among the elephants there was one who had the power of changing himself into a man. He agreed, therefore, to change his shape and go to visit the famous hunter. By conversation, the elephant was to learn the various stages through which the hunter passed, so that in one form or another he might be killed.

Accordingly, the elephant became a very handsome young man, and he went directly to the hunter's village. As it happened, the hunter had arrived home in good spirits for his evening meal, and he was surprised and pleased to welcome a stranger. As was the custom of his village, he invited the handsome stranger to share the meal and to spend the night under his roof.

It was but the matter of moments before the two learned that they shared an interest in hunting. And the hunter was pleased to be told that the stranger had come for no other reason than to talk with the man whose hunting skills had become known in the villages even beyond the great river. Dinner and a plentiful supply of palm wine loosened the men's tongues, until the elephant-man decided it would be safe to inquire about the famous hunter's changes in form. "How have you been able, in your daily hunting, to escape the dangers that take the lives of other hunters?" he asked. "I have heard that even a charging elephant has been powerless to harm you. How do you account for your remarkable escapes? Tell me. I am interested."

"Ah, my friend," said the hunter, "the case is more simple than you suspect. I am brave, it is true, but even the bravest man must yield to a charging elephant. And yield I do, but not in defeat. I merely change my shape."

"Oh? I am curious. Tell me more," urged the stranger. "How do you change your shape? And what forms do you take?"

"First I change to whispering grass," the hunter began. "Then, if the animal paws and tramples upon the grass, I change to a tall tree. If the animal should attack the tree, I become . . . " and he continued to tell the visitor of his various changes. "Of course, there must at last be an end to my changes," he concluded, "and if I should be attacked in the final form, I should forfeit my life. But my animal enemies would be unlikely to suspect what this is." He leaned closer to the stranger, ready to tell him of this final form, and the stranger waited eagerly to hear.

Now, the hunter's wife had been working quietly about the house as the men talked, and although she pretended not to listen, she was in truth quite anxious about her husband's giving away his secret to a stranger. She resolved to put an end to the conversation. As her husband said, "If all else should fail, I become . . . " his wife interrupted. "My dear," said she, "a wise man does not confide his secrets to a stranger. Nor should a man ever tell all he knows, even to his wife."

At that, the hunter suddenly realized how foolishly and freely he had talked. But was it too late? Had enough been said so that his life was endangered?

The stranger, annoyed that the hunter's wife had interrupted their conversation at such an important point, waited patiently for the hunter to continue his account. But the hunter, persuaded of his wife's good judgment, smiled and said, "Ah, but I am keeping you from your rest with all my talking. Both you and I must sleep well this night if we hope to hunt well tomorrow." And the guest was shown to his sleeping mat for the night.

Early on the morning of the following day, the visitor departed, and made his way into the heart of the bush country. There he returned to his form as an elephant.

One day as the hunter was seeking prey worthy of his skill, he came upon a large elephant. Raising his bow and fitting an arrow to the string, he prepared to shoot the animal. But to his surprise, the elephant turned and rushed toward him, trumpeting angrily. There was no time for the hunter to seek shelter, so he murmured his magic words and became of a sudden a patch of whispering grass.

But the elephant, in truth the visitor transformed, instantly began to trample the grass and to tear out great clumps of it with his trunk. Immediately the hunter whispered the magic words and suddenly became a straight, tall tree.

The elephant thereupon ran at the tree, encircled it with his powerful trunk, and exerted all his force to uproot it. Alarmed, the hunter changed from one form to another, but the elephant appeared each time to understand the change, and to be bent upon destroying the hunter before he could assume his final form.

Desperate, the hunter mumbled his magic words and became an *iromi*, a small water insect, skimming across the pond. Now, the elephant knew that the hunter had assumed another form, his final form, and that if he could be attacked in this form he could be destroyed forever, never more to harass the creatures of the bush country. But because the hunter's wife had interrupted their conversation, the elephant had been unable to learn exactly what that final form was. Perplexed, he struck out all about him with his trunk at whatever he suspected might be the hunter transformed. But in his anxiety he overlooked the *iromi*, that small creature amusing itself on the surface of the pond.

At last the elephant abandoned the search. He had come within a single step of victory, but that step was too long for even an elephant

possessed of certain magical powers to take. The hunter—man—
must forever continue to seek and destroy the bush-country beasts.
Disheartened, the elephant plunged into the forest to carry the word
to those creatures whose hopes had rested in him.

As for the hunter, as soon as the elephant had left, he changed
back through his various forms until he had returned to his shape as a
man. Recovering his bow and arrows, he hastened home to thank his
wife for preventing him from telling the stranger the secret on which
his life depended.

A LESSON FOR THE BAT

ONE DAY THE BAT planned to visit his father-in-law, who lived half a day's journey away. Unable to carry anything while he was flying, he asked a sheep if one of her lambs would carry his drinking horn for him. The mother sheep was none too willing to allow any of her lambs to go on such an errand, but as fortune would have it, the oldest lamb spoke up for himself.

"Let me go," he said quickly. "It will give me an occasion to learn something of the world. Come, Mother. Do let me go and help the bat." At length he was permitted to go.

Very early the next morning, the bat and the lamb set off together. After they had gone half the distance, the bat flew down to the roadside. "Stop here," said he, "and hide my drinking horn in the bush behind that palm tree."

Glad to be relieved of his troublesome load, the lamb left the drinking horn in the bush and the two went on toward the father-in-law's house. What with the gambolings of the lamb and the swoopings of the bat, the journey took them till well past noon.

No sooner had they arrived at the gate when the bat said, "Oh, my! I shall need my drinking horn. Surely you remember where you hid it?" And he sent the lamb back to fetch the drinking horn.

By the time the lamb had returned with the horn, the bat had eaten a fine dinner. "My, but you are slow!" he exclaimed. "If only you had hurried, you might have had some dinner, too. As it is, the dinner is all gone and we have already drunk our palm wine. There is nothing to do now but to take my drinking horn back and hide it in the bush again, where it will be safe. Next time, see that you are quicker about your business!"

The lamb hid the drinking horn in the bush again. Then, aching in every bone, he returned to the house to find supper already eaten. The cookpots were empty, and he was forced to go to bed hungry. By morning, he was indeed annoyed about the bat's behavior.

The next day, and the next, and the next, the bat followed the same policy, growing fat as the lamb grew thin. On the fifth day, the bat decided to return home, and he and the lamb set off. By the time they came to the bush where the drinking horn was hidden, the lamb was scarcely able to pick up the horn, he was so thin and weak. He finally arrived home, however, and he told the whole story to the mother sheep, complaining all the while of the terrible pain in his stomach.

The mother sheep, angry at the bat's mistreatment of her lamb, went to the tortoise, the wisest of all creatures, asking for some way in which she could take revenge on the bat. Patiently the tortoise listened to her story. He thought and thought. Finally he said, "Just leave the whole matter to me. I will teach him not to abuse others."

The next time the bat decided to visit his father-in-law, he went again to the sheep to ask for the help of her lamb. The tortoise, who happened along while the bat was there, said, "Why, I am going that way myself. I shall be happy to carry your drinking horn."

Early the next morning they set off together. When they had gone halfway, the bat flew down to the roadside. "Stop here," said he, "and hide my drinking horn in the bush behind that palm tree."

"Happily," said the tortoise, and he did as the bat directed. But the moment the bat flew off again, the tortoise picked up the drinking horn and hid it in the bag he was carrying. When they arrived at the house of the father-in-law, the tortoise hung the drinking horn at the back of a post in the yard and went inside to rest.

When it was time for dinner, the bat said, "Oh, my! I shall need my drinking horn. Surely you remember where you hid it?"

The tortoise remembered very well where he had left it. He went out into the yard, took the drinking horn from behind the post, and carried it in to the bat. In his annoyance at the tortoise's promptness, the bat refused to eat dinner, so the tortoise ate both his portion and the one that was meant for the bat. He found the meal very tasty.

The next day, and the next, and the next, the same thing happened, until the bat was unable to stand his hunger an hour longer. In fact, he was becoming as thin as the young lamb had been. Toward evening of the fourth day, he called his mother-in-law aside and whispered, "Without letting my friend the tortoise see you, please bring me a large meal. I shall take a nap while you prepare the food. And please hurry, for I am very hungry!"

Sitting silently in the corner, the tortoise overheard the bat's conversation with his mother-in-law. He waited until the bat had fallen sound asleep. Then he carried the bat very gently into his own bed-

room and returned to the bat's room, lying down under the bat's blanket. When the bat's mother-in-law had put the meal beside the bed, the tortoise quietly ate all but a tiny scrap of food and drank all but a scant spoonful of the delicious palm wine. After carrying the bat back, he placed the rest of the food and the palm wine between his lips. The tortoise then crept softly back to his own room to sleep.

When the bat awoke the next morning, he was nearly starved, and he was very angry with his mother-in-law because she had not prepared a meal for him.

"But I brought your food, just as you asked," she said. "And you ate it all. See, there is nothing left!"

"Indeed I did not!" retorted the bat crossly. "It must have been the tortoise who ate it."

"We can find out very quickly," said his mother-in-law. "We shall call the rest of the household, and they can decide whether you or someone else ate your dinner."

Meanwhile, the tortoise had gone to the father-in-law and persuaded him that the best way to find the thief would be to have both him and the bat rinse their mouths and spit out the water into separate calabashes. Then the tortoise quickly cleaned his teeth with his toothstick, rinsed his mouth thoroughly, and went back into the house.

When the bat's mother-in-law reported to the family the bat's complaint about the theft of his dinner, the father-in-law directed both the bat and the tortoise to rinse their mouths and to spit the water into separate basins. The water the tortoise spat out was clear and fresh, but the water the bat spat into his calabash had bits of food and traces of palm wine floating in it.

"Clearly my son-in-law ate his own dinner," said the mother-in-law, "and he has abused me for nothing. I do not care to have anything more to do with such a fellow. How can we ever trust him again?"

The entire household mocked the bat for attempting to cheat his own family. In fact, matters became so embarrassing that the bat hid himself away during the daytime, coming out only at night.

From that time, all bats have been nighttime creatures. Thus was the mother sheep avenged for the bat's mistreatment of her young lamb.

IT'S ALL THE FAULT OF ADAM

LONG AGO AND FAR AWAY there was a poor woodcutter named Iyapò. This Iyapò lived in the smallest hut of his village, and if he had been lazy he would have gone hungry to his mat at night.

But every morning he arose very early and went out well beyond his village to the forest. There the whole morning long he cut wood, good hard wood to make hot cooking fires. As soon as the sun shone high overhead, Iyapò loaded the wood on his shoulders and walked back along the highway and through the town gate, giving a few dry sticks to the gateman for his toll. Never mind how hungry he was. He must sell his firewood before he could buy even so much as a yam for his dinner.

"Wood! Wood!" he called as he walked up and down the winding streets. "It's all the fault of Adam. Wood! Good wood for sale!" And every day somehow he managed to sell his wood.

One day as Iyapò stopped in the market to cry, "Wood! Good wood for sale!" the *oba*, the king of the town, happened to hear him.

"Who is that man?" the king asked the *otun*, his chief adviser. "And what does he mean by saying, 'It's all the fault of Adam'?"

The *otun* asked the *osi*, and the *osi* asked the *balogun*, but none of the king's officers could answer the questions.

"Go, then," said the king to the *otun*, "and bring the woodcutter to me. If he has been unjustly treated, I must know about it."

As soon as Iyapò entered, he prostrated himself, laying first his right cheek and then his left cheek on the floor of the piazza where the king sat.

"Well," said the king, "I am curious. What is your name?"

"Sire," replied the woodcutter, shaking with dread, "my name is Iyapò."

"Iyapò . . . " the king murmured into the *Irù kèrè*. "Your name means 'many troubles.' But why must you blame *Adam* for your misfortunes?"

"S-sire," stammered Iyapò, "I have heard of Adam, who long ago disobeyed God and ate a certain fruit in the Garden of Eden. If Adam had not disobeyed, we would all be happy in the Garden. And I would not have to work so hard now to earn my daily food."

"Hmmn," said the king, looking long at the thin, ragged woodcutter. "You work hard, and you have but little. Surely it is unfair that someone else's disobedience should cause you so much grief. Something must be done for you.

"*Otun*," the king continued, "have Iyapò washed and dressed in clean, new clothes. Find a room somewhere in my palace where he can live. And take away his ragged clothes and his bundle of wood. From now on, he will lead a new and happy life."

Then, turning to the woodcutter, the king nodded. "From this day forward," he said, "you may call yourself my brother. Everything that I have you may share. You can do anything you want, except"—and he looked directly into Iyapò's eyes—"*except* open the green door near the end of the hall. That door you must never open."

"Oh, sire," answered Iyapò joyfully, "why should I want to open the green door? You have already given me everything I could want or need. I have food and clothing and shelter. Surely I should be contented!"

For many weeks the woodcutter enjoyed his good fortune. He ate three meals a day, instead of one. Indeed, he ate so well that he became fat. He wore the fine new clothes the king had given him. When he tired of these, the king's servants provided him with robes even more handsomely embroidered.

Day after day, week after week, he amused himself in the king's palace, until he had quite forgotten how it felt to arise early in the morning to cut wood. He no longer remembered the pain of hunger, or the sting of disappointment. He had almost forgotten that he had ever been anything else but the king's brother.

One day as he strolled through the palace, he chanced to notice the green door. "Ah," he murmured, "that is the door I must not open. How curious! I wonder what lies behind it?" But he knew he must not open it, so he turned his back upon it.

Day by day, however, he stopped often and oftener before the green door. Without his seeming to choose that hallway himself, his feet led him there, and he wondered more and more about what lay behind the door. Each time he came closer to putting his hand upon the latch, but still he hesitated.

Then one day the king was called to another part of the town on business. "Iyapò, my brother," he said, "look after the palace in my absence. I may not be back until well past dinner time."

"Look after the palace," Iyapò murmured as the king left the compound. "If I am to look after the palace, surely I am responsible for the room behind the green door. After all, I am the king's brother. Why should *any* room be forbidden to me?" Looking carefully here and there to be sure he was not watched, Iyapò went quietly to the green door. He listened, with his ear pressed against the door. There was not a sound from the other side. I'll open it just a little bit," he decided, "and then I'll close it tightly again. The king will never know. But I *must* discover what is inside."

Lifting the latch, he peered into the room. He blinked, and looked again. There was nothing at all in the room except his own ragged clothes and his bundle of wood! As he stood there, disbelieving, a small gray mouse hiding in a shadow in the far corner suddenly ran between Iyapò's feet and out into the hallway. "Ah!" exclaimed Iyapò. "It must be the *mouse* that the king is so careful about! I must catch him and put him back, or the king will know that I have opened the green door." Hastily latching the door, he set out after the mouse.

Up one hallway and down another raced Iyapò, with the mouse in sight but just beyond his reach. Soon he began to huff and puff. All those weeks of good eating had made him too fat to run easily. And he stumbled again and again on the wide skirt of the handsome robe he was wearing. Pausing a moment, he took off the robe and flung it on a bench. Then he ran again, faster, losing his right shoe here, his left shoe there. *Still* he could not catch the little gray mouse.

"What are you doing?" The voice of the king rang through the hall.

Iyapò stopped running. His heart pounded till it seemed as if the very walls must hear it. The king! But he was not to return until well past dinner time . . . Suddenly Iyapò knew fear. He fell to his knees before the king.

"Oh, sire," he began, "I am sorry about your mouse."

"My *mouse?*" the king asked, puzzled. "I have no mouse. And what are you doing, running through the palace without your robe, without your shoes? The brother of the king must walk proudly, with dignity."

"You—you see, my brother," Iyapò stammered, "the mouse ran out when I opened the green door, and I knew that—"

"The green door!" exclaimed the king. "So you opened the green door. Was that not the *one thing* I told you that you must not do?"

"Oh, yes, sire, it *was,*" Iyapò agreed. "And I wasn't going to open it. But day after day it was there, and day after day I wondered about it. And as the king's brother—"

"As the king's brother," the king interrupted, his eyes blazing with anger, "you felt you must be the king himself. And you thought *Adam* was disobedient! What *he* did should have taught you caution."

Iyapò prostrated himself before the king, right cheek on the floor, left cheek on the floor. Then, "What is your will, O king?" he whispered.

"Go to the green door," said the king, his voice low now, and sorrowful. "Take your ragged clothes and your bundle of wood. It is not other people's good wishes which can make you happy, but your own destiny. Sell your wood, since work is the cure for poverty. But know this, my friend: your misfortune is not the fault of Adam."

Iyapò arose. He walked on his bare feet past the fine shoes he had lost, past the handsome robe he had flung aside, to the green door. Opening it, he put on his ragged clothes, which scarcely covered his stout figure. Lifting the bundle of wood to his shoulders, he walked out of the cool palace into the dust and heat of the market. "Wood! Wood for sale!" he called. "Wood! Good wood for sale!" But no matter how many times he cried his "Wood for sale!" there was no longer a mention of Adam.

TORTOISE AND BABARINSA'S DAUGHTERS

FAR AWAY AND LONG AGO in a small village lived a humble but respectable family. Though this family had no wealth, they had three beautiful daughters, the most beautiful girls in the entire kingdom. No man could set eyes on them without desiring one for his wife. As for Babarinsa and his wife, they would sooner have parted with their eyes than with their daughters.

The rich and the poor, the noble and the lowly, the old and the young came seeking the hand of one or another of the lovely girls. To each suitor, Babarinsa had but one thing to say: "Irrespective of appearance, wealth, or social standing, the one who can declare in public meeting the names of my three daughters may have them all as wives." For well the father knew that none in all the kingdom, even the king himself, knew the names of Babarinsa's daughters. The parents never called their daughters by name outside their own gate, and they lived without neighbors at the very edge of the village. How *could* anyone learn the names of the girls?

But Tortoise, on hearing Babarinsa's proclamation, determined to find out for himself the names of these beautiful girls. By inquiring here and there, he discovered where Babarinsa and his family lived. Day after day he watched the movements of the girls very closely without allowing himself to be seen. After a short time he knew Babarinsa's garden as well as he knew his own house, and besides that, he knew that every evening before sunset the girls entertained themselves in the garden.

One evening Tortoise gathered three beautiful and unusual bouquets. Climbing a tree overlooking Babarinsa's garden, Tortoise watched the three girls amusing themselves. Then he tossed one of the bouquets to the ground near one of the girls. Noticing the bouquet, the girl ran and snatched it up, calling to her sisters,

Come see my flowers,
Opobipobi, Oripolobi!

Running to their sister, the two girls exclaimed over the beautiful bouquet. While they were still admiring it, Tortoise dropped a second bouquet near one of the other two sisters. This sister, spying the flowers, ran and snatched them up, crying to her sisters,

Come see my flowers,
Ajobikobi, Oripolobi!

At once Ajobikobi and Oripolobi ran to her side to see this new and different bouquet. A moment later, Tortoise dropped the third bouquet near Oripolobi, who ran at once to pick it up. Holding it close to her, she sang,

Come see my flowers,
Ajobikobi, Opobipobi!

In this fashion, Tortoise learned not only the three names but to which of the daughters each name belonged. He sat patiently in the tree until the girls had left the garden. Then slowly and carefully he climbed down the tree and went home.

Early the following morning Tortoise arose and went to visit the king. "Sire," said he, "it is time to call a public meeting. I, the humble Tortoise, have learned the names of Babarinsa's daughters."

The king stared at Tortoise in disbelief. Then, remembering what he had heard of the cleverness of Tortoise, the king began to reason with him. "Tortoise, my friend," he said, "since you cannot *dream* of having Babarinsa's daughters for yourself, suppose you tell *me* the names." For in truth the king himself wished to marry the girls.

But Tortoise was not to be persuaded, for with every tempting offer the king laid before him in exchange for the information—money, gems, position—Babarinsa's daughters grew in beauty, until Tortoise resolved to claim the girls for himself.

At last the king became suspicious that Tortoise was deceiving him. In order to expose the deception, he announced that on a certain day there would be a meeting of all the people in his kingdom. At that time, anyone who felt certain he knew the names of Babarinsa's daughters would be free to try his claim. If the claimant *did* know the names, well and good; he would be awarded the three beautiful girls as his brides. On the other hand, if his claims were false, the claimant would be exposed to the ridicule of the entire community.

When the day came, all the people assembled, including Babarinsa and his three beautiful daughters. All were curious to see what would become of Babarinsa's daughters. When all were silent, the king arose. "We have met today," he began, "to see who among us knows the names of Babarinsa's daughters. Will anyone who feels certain he knows the names of these beautiful girls please step forward."

For a moment after the king had ceased speaking, there was perfect silence. Then, one by one, people turned to look at their neighbors, wondering who would be so bold as to state his claim. When no one else stepped forward, Tortoise arose and walked slowly toward the king. Some among the audience laughed; some jeered; some looked surprised; still others, knowing Tortoise's reputation for wisdom, waited eagerly to see whether this time Tortoise had at last overstepped himself.

Reaching a spot at the king's feet, Tortoise prostrated himself before the king. Then, raising his head erect, he faced the audience.

"My brothers, sisters, and friends," he began solemnly, "this is a significant day, and it gives me great pleasure to appear thus before you. I am ready to give the names of Babarinsa's three beautiful daughters."

A murmur among the audience grew louder and louder. Then, as Tortoise raised his paw, a silence fell upon the throng. Pointing to one of the girls as he spoke, Tortoise said, "The name of the first girl is Ajobikobi. The name of the second," and he pointed to another, "is Opobipobi. And the third is named Oripolobi," he concluded, pointing to the third daughter.

Babarinsa and his wife, who had smiled scornfully when Tortoise had risen to make his claim, looked at one another aghast. To the king's query, "Babarinsa, is Tortoise right?" the father had to answer, "Yes." Reluctantly he gave his daughters over to Tortoise, who of all the community was the only one entirely pleased by the business which had been enacted that day.

Amid a stunned silence, Tortoise left the gathering with his three wives, Ajobikobi, Opobipobi, and Oripolobi. As he led them toward his home beyond the river, the sisters talked among themselves, weeping all the while, and mourning the earlier fine proposals which their father had so grandly refused. At length Ajobikobi, filled with despair, stopped to lean for a moment against the lowest branch of a great tree. Crying out that she would rather lose her life than be Tortoise's wife, she became a leaf among the hundreds of other leaves on the tree, indistinguishable from the rest.

Tortoise, astounded by the loss of his first wife, attempted at once to find her. Failing that, he consoled himself with the knowledge that at least he had two beautiful wives left.

As Tortoise and the other two continued on their way, Opobipobi

also became overwhelmed by sorrow and despair. Flinging herself down among the ferns along the river, she cried out that she would rather die than be counted among the wives of the lowly Tortoise. Of a sudden, she became a fern herself, one among many others exactly like herself along the riverbank.

Tortoise, gripped with fear and horror, scrambled among the ferns in a frantic attempt to recover his second wife. But, alas, he was unable to find her.

Then, determined at least to arrive home with one of his wives, Tortoise grasped Oripolobi's skirt, intending to prevent her from leaping into the river and drowning herself in her great grief. But the moment he touched her, she turned into water and flowed away, a part of the silver river.

Alone now, Tortoise was saddened with the outcome of what had been a splendid triumph, and overwhelmed with distaste for the false pride which had lain at the root of his claim to Babarinsa's daughters. He fled into the forest, never again to look upon the faces of those who could know his shame and despair. And Tortoise still hides today lest others taunt him with the vanity of his unnatural ambition.

TEST OF A FRIENDSHIP

ONG AGO AND FAR AWAY there were two good friends named Olaleye and Omoteji. Each had a farm directly across the footpath from the other, and day after day they would greet each other as they went about their work. Finally their great friendship raised a question in the heart of their wise neighbor, and he determined to test their friendship for one another.

Secretly, he made a hat for himself which was red on one side and green on the other. Then one day after putting on his new hat, he strolled along the footpath.

"Good morning!" he greeted Omoteji as the good fellow bent over the yams in his field.

"Good morning," answered Omoteji, standing up to stretch himself a little from his bending. "I see you have a fine new red hat."

"Oh, yes," answered the other. "I am happy that you noticed it."

And he set his new hat more firmly upon his head. He walked on along the footpath, and Omoteji returned to his work.

A few moments later, he saw Olaleye pulling weeds in his yam patch. "Good morning, Olaleye!" he called.

Olaleye looked up and returned the man's greeting. Then, "Oho," said he. "I see you have a fine new green hat."

"Yes, indeed," answered the neighbor. "I looked a long time before I found the one I wanted." After a moment's chatting with Olaleye, he went on his way down the footpath, well satisfied with himself.

When the sun stood at the zenith, Olaleye stopped his work and went to eat his lunch with his good friend Omoteji. As they ate, Omoteji said, "Did you notice the fine new red hat our neighbor had?"

"*Red* hat!" exclaimed Olaleye. "My friend, you must have been a little dazzled by the sun."

"What do you mean?" asked Omoteji.

"It wasn't a red hat our neighbor was wearing. It was a *green* hat," explained Olaleye. And he smiled at his friend's mistake.

"A green hat!" exclaimed Omoteji. "Oh, no, my friend. It was *not* green. It was red. I know, for I remarked on it to our neighbor."

"And so did I," returned Olaleye, becoming a little impatient.

Omoteji, irritated by his friend's impatience, continued to argue that the hat was red, while Olaleye for his part maintained that the hat was green. From words, the quarrel grew to blows, and Omoteji was still reeling from Olaleye's stout blow when their neighbor hurried toward them.

"What's this!" he exclaimed. "You two fighting! I thought you were the best of friends. How can friends come to blows this way?"

Olaleye and Omoteji, their excitement somewhat cooled by this interruption, stared at their neighbor. This time, Omoteji saw the green side of the hat, and Olaleye saw the red side.

"Oh, my friend Omoteji," said Olaleye quickly. "You were right, after all. Our neighbor's hat *is* red."

"Oh, no," returned Omoteji earnestly. "I was wrong and you were right.. I must have been dazzled by the sun, after all. Our neighbor's new hat is green."

Their difference of opinion would shortly have led to blows again if their neighbor had not laughed. Taking off his hat, he showed them the red side and then the green one. "Look here, my friends," he said. "You were both right about the hat. But you were both wrong about your friendship. You are not the best of friends if you cannot examine both sides of a question without anger, whether it be a hat or whether it be something more important."

"You are right," declared Olaleye. "One never knows about a friendship until it has been put to a test. As for me, a hat can be either green or red. It doesn't matter, as long as I have my good friend, Omoteji."

"Nor does it matter to me," agreed Omoteji.

And thenceforth the two were stronger friends than ever.

THE BOY AND THE LEOPARD

LONG AGO AND FAR AWAY there was a wealthy man who had several wives. Of a sudden, this man learned that his town was to be invaded by men from another tribe. Fearing for his life and the lives of those in his family, the man thought long about what he must do to save them all. Finally he decided that he and his family would leave the town under cover of darkness, and seek safety for themselves in the land at the other side of the forest. Accordingly, that night he gathered together his wives and all their children. Packing up whatever possessions they were able to carry, the party started out through the forest.

Now, the man's favorite wife was soon to bear a child, and she found traveling through the forest very difficult. Despite her husband's urging, she walked more and more slowly, until finally she could go not a single step farther.

Her husband halted in his flight, uncertain of what to do about his wife. If he left her there alone, she would without question be torn apart by wild beasts. On the other hand, if he kept the whole party together, traveling only as fast as this wife could go, they would all be captured and enslaved by the enemy tribe. At last he decided that he must leave his wife to face her own fate, and he went off through the forest with the rest of his family.

The following day, a boy was born to the abandoned wife. Taking her baby, the woman went deeper into the forest and found a place safe from the enemy tribe and from wild animals. There she cared for her child, going out from her shelter only to seek food and clothing for herself and the boy. As the boy grew, he played with the small animals of the forest, each day wandering a little farther away from his mother's protection.

One day while he was playing in the forest he found a leopard cub. They approached each other timidly, but soon, as is the way with young creatures, they were good friends. All day they played in a sunny place in the forest, and when the boy had to leave the cub and go back to his mother, he promised the cub that he would return the following day to play with him. At length the two discovered that they had been born the same year and that each had a mother as his sole protection. When the boy seemed fearful that the cub's mother would kill his own mother, the cub promised to kill meat for the boy and his mother so that the woman need not risk her life by going out to hunt.

One day, however, the young leopard came home to find his mother standing over the body of the woman, who had gone out to seek water and had been brought down by the mother leopard. Grief-stricken,

the cub went in search of the boy and, telling him what had happened, he promised to take care of the boy so that he would suffer neither hunger nor harm.

After that, he took the boy to live with him in his own cave. Day after day, the two became closer friends, until they almost forgot that one was a leopard and the other a boy.

The cub noticed one day that his friend was very sad. After much coaxing, the boy told the cub what was troubling him. "Long ago my mother told me that when I was old enough I should offer a sacrifice to the gods so that I might have a life filled with joy and contentment. I am now old enough, but I am unable to get the proper things to offer in sacrifice."

"What do you need?" asked the young leopard.

"My mother said I must offer snails, kola nuts, and palm nuts. But such things are beyond my means. They are sold in the marketplace. How am I to get the money for such a purpose?" the boy asked sadly.

"Do not worry," said the leopard. "I shall go to the market myself and get them for you." Despite the boy's urging, the cub would not reveal the plan he had for getting the goods from the marketplace.

On the following market day, the leopard arose very early and quietly left the cave. Going to the marketplace, he climbed a tree overlooking the market and hid himself there. By midday, the marketplace was thronged with people. Suddenly the leopard leaped down into the midst of the crowd. The people fled far and wide in their panic. Calmly the leopard chose those things which the boy needed for his sacrifice and he returned with them to the cave. The next day, the boy offered a sacrifice to appease his gods.

Not long after that, the boy again looked sad. "What is the matter now, my friend?" the leopard inquired.

The boy sighed. "I need clothes. But how am I to find something suitable to wear?"

"Clothes?" puzzled the leopard. "I do not see why you need clothes, my friend, but if you need them, I shall get them for you." Going to the market on the following market day, the leopard again frightened the crowds away from the stalls and brought back some fine clothes for the boy.

Some time later, the leopard, noting that the boy looked sad and woebegone, asked what was troubling him. The boy sighed deeply. "My friend," said he, "it is the custom among men to marry. But how am I to find a bride?"

"A bride? Why do you need a bride? Am I not a sufficient friend for you?" asked the leopard.

"Ah, indeed, you are the best friend I could ever have," the boy assured him. "All the same, I feel a great longing for a wife. Do not worry, my friend," the boy added. "My having a wife will never be permitted to interfere with our friendship." Comforted thus, the leopard agreed to help the boy seek a wife.

On the very next market day the two friends dressed themselves in some of the clothes which the leopard had brought back for the boy, and then they walked to the marketplace. As they approached the center of the market, they saw a very beautiful girl. The boy looked after her with longing, and the leopard resolved to capture the girl as a wife for his friend. To capture her would take much doing, for she was the only daughter of the king. Nonetheless, the leopard was determined to please the boy, and he thought and thought about the matter until finally he had arrived at a plan.

"Listen carefully," he said to the boy. "On the next market day I shall go to the market, kill the girl, and refuse to release her body for burial to anyone but you. Then you will squeeze into the eyes of the princess several drops of juice from a certain leaf I shall get from the forest for you. With this juice you will be able to bring the girl back to life. The king will surely give his daughter to you when he sees how brave and skillful you are."

The boy was pleased with the leopard's plan, and he promised to follow his friend's directions exactly. On the following market day, the leopard did exactly as he had planned to do: he killed the princess and then he stood over her body, refusing to permit even the bravest of the king's soldiers to recover the body for burial. Suddenly the boy appeared in the marketplace and went directly to the king. "Sire," said he, "if you will permit me to marry the princess afterwards, I shall not only recover her body from the leopard, but I shall bring her back to life."

The king stared in disbelief at the young stranger. Finally he promised his daughter's hand to the boy if he could do all that he had claimed. The boy, after reciting some incantations, walked boldly up to the leopard, stooped down, and picked up the body of the princess. Without a sound, the leopard fled into the forest. Then the boy, laying the princess down gently at her father's feet, squeezed several drops of the magic juice directly into her eyes. Rumors had taken wing that the princess was to be revived, and the crowd pressed in upon the two, eager to see whether the princess would indeed recover.

The moment the juice had entered the eyes of the princess, she blinked and then sat up and looked around. "What am I doing here?" she asked. "And why have all these people gathered here?"

The king, astounded and pleased beyond measure at the recovery of his daughter, told her what had happened. Then, true to his promise, he gave his daughter to the boy in marriage. In a matter of weeks he built for them a beautiful house with a garden extending clear to the edge of the forest.

The night after the boy and his bride had moved into their new home, the boy slipped away into the forest to tell the leopard all that had happened and to urge him to come every night and meet with him in the end of the garden right near the forest. The leopard, rejoicing that the boy's marriage would not interrupt their friendship, began coming every night to the garden to visit his friend. At length the girl noticed her husband's absence and, wondering what he could be finding to do in the garden in the middle of the night, she followed him to find out for herself. To her astonishment, she found her husband at the lower end of the garden talking with a large leopard. Fearful that harm would come to him, she was just about to scream for help when her husband saw her and motioned to her to be silent. He explained then that he and the leopard had been friends since childhood and that she must not fear the leopard, since he would be coming each night as a visitor. Despite her horror and surprise, the girl agreed to accept the leopard as a friend of the family.

But fear is not easily dismissed. Although the girl wished to please her husband, she became steadily more uneasy about the leopard's visits. Finally she slipped away one day to visit her parents, and when they detected that something was troubling her, she wept and told them of her husband's strange friend. Her father at once suspected that this was the animal which had killed his daughter in the market-place. "He may be a friend of your husband's, but he is no friend of yours," her father said. "The leopard must be destroyed."

At once the king summoned a dozen of his most trusted palace guards. "Go this evening at sunset," he instructed them, "and lie in wait at the lower end of my daughter's garden until you see a leopard enter. Kill him and return to me." As for his daughter, he kept her at the palace, where she would be safe until the leopard had been dis-posed of.

That evening the leopard came a little earlier than the usual time. To his surprise, he was met by a shower of poisoned arrows. He ran back toward the forest, but he had been fatally wounded, and shortly

afterwards he died. The guards were satisfied that he had been destroyed, and they returned to the palace to carry their report to the king.

When the boy arrived at the appointed place, he was surprised not to see the leopard. A trail of blood led him to the edge of the forest, where his friend lay dead. As the boy knelt to examine the leopard for any faint signs of life, he became aware that some creature was watching him. It was the tortoise, who had chanced to see the close of the leopard's life. Weeping, the boy begged the tortoise to find him one of the magic leaves, that he might restore life to his friend. After much persuasion, the tortoise led him to a plant bearing the magic leaves. Quickly breaking off a leaf, the boy went to the leopard and squeezed a few drops of the juice into his eyes.

As soon as he had opened his eyes, the leopard reproached the boy for his unkind treatment.

"Ah, but I was not the one who shot you," the boy assured him, "nor do I know why you were shot."

"My friends," the tortoise said, "do not blame men for this action. Your fellowship does not fit the world of men. And even in the world of animals it is unusual enough so that many will strive to destroy it. The time is past for your friendship. Return each to your own world and be content."

Cutting a palm branch, the tortoise tore it apart before them in the age-old symbol of separation. Heavy with grief, the leopard turned and went off into the forest. The boy watched sadly until he could no longer see the leopard among the trees. Then he turned and walked through his garden and into the world of men. From that day, men and wild animals ceased to be friends.

THE REWARD OF TREACHERY

LONG AGO AND FAR AWAY there were two good friends who chanced to work in the same shop. As time passed, the more hardworking man of the two was promoted to a higher position in the shop, and the other one became very jealous. At last, unable to tolerate his friend's good fortune any longer, the envious friend consulted a *babalawo* (native priest) to see what he might get that would rid him of his friend.

On hearing what was wanted, the *babalawo* had many misgivings. "Such methods should be used with great caution," he warned. "He who does evil to others injures himself. Unless this man has truly done you great harm, you should not treat him in this way."

But the jealous one insisted that his friend had proved unfaithful, and by claims of this and that injustice he persuaded the *babalawo* of the truth of his injury. At last the priest agreed to his request, and prepared for him a potent poison. "Take this poison," he said, "and place it under the cushion of the chair on which your enemy sits. After he has sat on the potion for a few moments, his body will begin to decay, although his mind will still be active. He will not die at once, but he will suffer such torment that he will be forced to take to his bed for the last few days of his life. Remember, though: this is a very powerful potion. Do not use it without thought of the consequences."

The envious one greedily took the parcel, and, promising to use it with care, he hurried away. Concealing the packet, he went to work the following morning much earlier than usual. Seeing no one else in the shop, he hid the packet under the cushion on his friend's chair. Then he bustled about, humming to himself, straightening a chair here and there, and even dusting a shelf or two. His friend, arriving a few moments later, was surprised to find someone there ahead of him. "Aha, my friend! Is it really you?" he exclaimed. "You are becoming more industrious in your habits." But the more he watched the unusual industry of his habitually lazy friend, the more suspicious he became. Instead of seating himself immediately at his desk, as his friend invited him to do, he invented an errand on which he could send the man, so that he could find out for himself what this unusual bustle was about.

Although the guilty man did not wish to leave the shop for a moment, eager as he was to see the potion begin its deadly work, still he had to go, since the other one was his superior in the shop. While he was hurrying along about the errand, his friend looked here and there around the shop to determine whether there had been anything stolen, or whether there had been any changes made at all. Noting that the cushion on his chair was awry, he picked it up to look under it, and there he saw a peculiar packet. Not knowing what it was, but

assuming that his friend had put it there, he put it under his friend's cushion.

He had just sat down in his own chair when the jealous man rushed into the shop, the errand having been completed. The jealous one smiled with satisfaction at seeing his friend at last seated at the desk and at work. He busied himself at his own desk, impatient to see the first signs that the magic potion had begun to work. But as he sat, he began to feel a dizziness and then a pain. Suddenly he realized that his own trick had been turned upon him. He was the victim of his own abuse. Dreading to learn the truth, yet needing to know, he sat impatiently until his friend had left to eat lunch. When no one else remained in the shop, the jealous man leaped from his chair and feverishly snatched off the cushion. Just as he had feared, there lay the packet.

Forgetting everything else in his pain and grief, the wretched man ran to the priest. "Help me! Help me!" he cried. "I myself have become the victim of that potion you gave me."

But the *babalawo* just shook his head. "I am sorry, my friend," he said, "but there is nothing I can do to halt the work of the potion. It is beyond my power to undo the evil which you have begun. You have made your choice; now you must live with it."

In despair, the jealous one turned his footsteps homeward. Unable to bear the pain and unable to find a cure for it, he took to his bed and spent his last few days in torment, his body decaying while his mind taunted him about his treachery toward his friend. At last death came to relieve him, a victim of his own hand. In just such a fashion does treachery reward itself.

GLOSSARY

Glossary

ADAM: With the introduction of Christianity into Western Nigeria came the story of the Garden of Eden. In his *Inside Africa*, John Gunther quotes a passage from the Yorubas' pidgin-English version of the Adam and Eve story. The Garden of Eden had "plenty beef, plenty cassava, plenty banana, plenty yam, plenty guinea corn, plenty mango, plenty groundnut" [peanuts]. The tree at the center of the garden was the mango, forbidden to the black man but reserved for the white man. When questioned by God, Adam said the woman had used the mangoes in a "groundnut stew." Translated into such terms, the story of Adam would undoubtedly make a strong impression on Iyapò in "It's All the Fault of Adam," and he might well think to blame all his troubles on Adam, that first disobedient child of God.

AMO: In "The Dancing Palm Tree," the clay image called Sigidi was coated with *amo*, or birdlime, a very sticky substance taken from the breadfruit tree and usually spread on twigs to snare small birds. Very much the same trick was used to catch Brer Rabbit in the Tar-Baby story of Joel Chandler Harris.

BAT: There are many folktales about the bat told by the Yorubas, most of them purporting to explain why the bat comes out only at night. "A Lesson for the Bat" is by all odds the most entertaining bat story known to Ola Idewu.

BELLMAN: In "Ashoremashika," the victim of the snake is the bellman, a very familiar figure in Yoruba towns and villages. The bellman serves as the king's messenger, carrying the news to all the people whenever the king wants to make a proclamation, to recruit soldiers, or to summon certain individuals to his palace. With him the bellman carries two bells, a small one and a large one, fastened side by side and struck alternately with quick blows. The last three beats come on the small bell, marking the end of the signal. Then the bellman very solemnly and clearly announces what he has been sent to say.

BUSH RATS: The bush rats hunted by Tortoise in "The Dancing Palm Tree" are similar to our wood rats, with soft fur, light grayish above and white below. In Western Nigeria there is a great shortage of meat, and even a wood rat would sometimes seem an attractive addition to the diet.

The Dancing Palm Tree

The good hunter is highly respected because of the great difficulty in finding game. The forest in which he hunts is known as "the bush," a term used to refer to uncleared or untilled districts which are still naturally covered by trees and shrubs.

Though Nigeria has a tropical climate, the forest there is not *jungle;* Nigerians are quite indignant when outsiders refer to their tropical rain forest as "jungle." These forests contain a fine source of wealth for Nigeria in their hardwood trees, especially mahogany and obeche (also called *arere* and *wawa*). Half of the timber exported from Nigeria is obeche, which is very light and workable for a hardwood. It is one of the tallest trees in the forest, and up to five feet in diameter.

Especially common and valuable are the oil palm, the kola tree, and the cacao; these trees furnish the bulk of Nigeria's exports. Whenever we use a soap with a palm-oil base, or drink a cola beverage, or sip a cup of cocoa, the chances are good that we are using something sent originally from Nigeria.

CALABASH: The calabash is a gourd which is useful to the Yorubas in many ways. Large ones are cut in half to make trays and basketlike containers; small ones are used as bowls or basins; still smaller ones are used as spoons. They can be used plain, or they can be handsomely carved and decorated. The town of Oyo is famous for its white rubbed, intricately carved calabash bowls.

The term "calabash" is used also to refer to the king's chief aides; those next to him in authority—the *otun,* the *ona,* and the *osi*—are known as "the first calabash to the king," "the second calabash to the king," and "the third calabash to the king."

In addition, calabashes, when thoroughly dried, make fine rattles to use in processions and to accompany dancing and various festivals.

FARMER: The Nigerians are almost entirely dependent upon agriculture for their income. Though they choose to live in villages, towns, and cities because they are a sociable people, they still work their farms to earn their living, sometimes walking or riding great distances each day to go to work.

In his farm lot, which rarely measures more than two or three acres, the farmer raises chiefly yams, collard greens, cassava (the source of tapioca), guinea corn, breadfruit, rice, okra, and fruits of various kinds, including mangoes and pawpaws (melons). The work on these farms is done by all the family members, with the children very early learning to do their share of hoeing, weeding, and digging. The implements, even to this day, are very simple; the chief tools of the farmer are his hoe, his axe, and his cutlass. Plowing is almost unknown, and the shortage of draft animals reduces the likelihood that plowing will be introduced.

Yams are especially popular as a food product because they grow well and are nourishing, and can be served in so many ways; pounded yam made into *foofoo*, highly spiced with chili powder and peppers, is one of the favorite foods in Yorubaland. Fish and such game as can be caught, plus chickens and goats, furnish the slender amount of animal protein in the West Nigerians' diet.

GREAT CEREMONY: When the king went to the marketplace, in "The Dancing Palm Tree," he went "with great ceremony." In such a processional the king, shaded by his immense, gold-fringed umbrella, would be accompanied by his whole court. Preceding him would be drummers and "fifers," the drummers bearing drums of all shapes and sizes, but most interesting among them the "talking drums." These are carried under the drummers' arms, with the drum stroked or squeezed to produce various tones, so that the drums actually sound as if they are speaking. Other drums are made of clay pots with holes bored in them; others are of wood, with drumheads of skin. Accompanying the drummers are musicians blowing on horns and flutes and trumpets, some made from the horns of goats and sheep and some from the tusks of elephants. Still other musicians carry calabash rattles.

IRÙ KÈRÈ: In "It's All the Fault of Adam," the king "murmured into the *Irù kèrè.*" The *Irù kèrè* is a specially prepared white cow's tail which is held before his mouth by the king whenever he speaks, since it is considered unseemly for him to be seen opening his mouth in public. He speaks very softly into the *Irù kèrè*, and his words are repeated loudly by his spokesman, the *ona*. In addition to this function, the *Irù kèrè* serves as a symbol of grace and peace.

Besides the *Irù kèrè*, the king has an *Ejigba*, or "chain of office," made of expensive beads which goes around his neck and hangs to the knees, and a scepter called the *Opa Ilekè*, which is entirely covered by small varicolored beads.

The Dancing Palm Tree

MAGIC: Tortoise in "The Dancing Palm Tree" has a magical gift that enables him to cause a palm tree to dance, roots and all, away from its place in the forest.

Very close to magic in this and other tales are medicines and potions: the powder used by Ashoremashika to revive the king's daughter, the juice from the leaf which healed the leopard, and the potion which the jealous man hoped to use to take the life of his ambitious and hardworking friend. Both magic and magical potions are very much a part of Yoruba life today, despite the fact that Nigerian law now provides specific penalties for "juju," witchcraft, and criminal charms. The *jujuman* is a frequent sight in cities, towns, and villages, walking through the crowded streets bearing his stock in trade, or operating in the marketplace in a stall hung with monkey skulls, dried mice impaled on sticks, parrot beaks, snake fangs, cuttlebones, seashells, magical seeds, roots and barks, and herbs of all kinds.

The *babalawo*, or native priest, whose traffic in such charms and cures is highly regarded, is sought out by those desiring to work evil against their neighbors, as well as by those seeking cures for themselves. Thus the jealous man consulted the *babalawo* for a potion to destroy the life of his unsuspecting friend.

The Yoruba kings in some instances have special groups of "witch doctors" at their service when they find it advisable to dispose of an enemy. These men are protected by the king, but in return they are expected to be dependable in their magic. If the potion prepared by one of these "doctors" fails to accomplish the end of destroying the enemy, the "doctor" pays with his own life for his faulty judgment.

MARKETPLACE: The marketplace furnishes for the Yorubas both an important social center and the means by which they can obtain the few articles they consider necessary to supplement what they produce on their farms. Market day in the average market is held every fourth day, and it is the occasion for a full day of trading and chatter. The market may be large or small—some serve only their immediate villages, while others draw people from hundreds of miles around—but they all have several features in common: 1. they are noisy and colorful; 2. the range of goods offered is tremendous; 3. most of the tradespeople have carried to market on their heads the goods they hope to sell that day; 4. there are no fixed prices, but extensive bargaining until a satisfactory price is reached.

Articles bought are paid for in cowries (shell money arranged in strings), or in

British coins (pence, shillings, and pounds), or in goods of equal value exchanged for the ones purchased. The Yorubas (especially the women) are very fond of trading, and are very clever at completing a trade.

Invariably, there is a marketplace in front of the king's palace, and there is likely to be a small market at the door of a smaller chief's house. This is one of the privileges of the ruler: to have the busiest scene of the town right on his own doorstep. Tradespeople call their wares, in an effort to entice buyers. Thus the king in "It's All the Fault of Adam" would have heard the woodcutter's complaint, since it was cried out right beneath his window. The marketplace in "The Dancing Palm Tree" must have been a regional market, not one located before the king's palace, for the king was not aware of the dancing palm until the villagers appealed to him for help.

NO-KING-IS-AS-GREAT-AS-GOD: Names such as this one are quite common in Yoruba life. In fact, the whole process of naming is an extremely interesting and complicated one. Each name which is used has a definite meaning and purpose, and it tells a great deal about its owner.

A child may have as many as three names at the time of his naming ceremony, or christening (on the ninth day of life for a boy, on the seventh day for a girl):

1. a name specifying his position in the family or some special condition under which he was born; for example, The-First-Born, Born-After-His-Father-Died, or Born-with-Curly-Hair.

2. a christening name chosen by someone present at the christening to show something about the family or about the child; for example, A-Child-Big-Enough-for-Two, I-Have-Someone-to-Pet, or Many-Trials.

3. a name showing his totem, or his birth line. (Children take their father's totem unless their mother's totem is of higher rank, in which case they can be given their mother's totem.) There is a different totem for each family line; for example, Elephant, Post, God of War, or Love-Bird. A fourth name—an attributive or pet name—is given to the child at a later time; this name describes what the child is or what it is hoped he will become; for example, One-Who-Possesses-After-a-Struggle, or One-Who-Causes-Joy-All-Around. Adults call children by their pet names, but children are not permitted to use pet names when

speaking to or about adults. Interestingly, most Yoruba names can be used either for boys or for girls, so just by the name you usually cannot tell whether a child is a girl or a boy.

Babarinsa's name in "Tortoise and Babarinsa's Daughters" is perhaps a corruption of *Babarimisa*, meaning Born-After-His-Father-Died.

The name No-King-Is-as-Great-as-God would be a christening name, not a pet name, and it would reveal the family's firm belief in the omnipotence of God. Since names are considered very significant in Nigeria, the king could be expected to be irritated by such a name in the possession of a common man.

Iyapò's name is a christening name referring to the family's condition (Many-Trials). The king in "It's All the Fault of Adam" recognized that Iyapò's troubles were presumably those he had been born with, and not his fault at all; that is why he gave Iyapò the chance to change his luck.

Ashoremashika is a pet name showing the kindly character of the farmer.

OBA: The king in a Yoruba city or town or village is known as the *oba*. In addition, he may carry another name showing the source of his title: the Alake of Abeokuta and the Alafin of Oyo, for example. Kingship among the Yorubas is not hereditary; a Council or Senatorial Society (*Ogboni*) act as counselors to the king, and serve as "kingmakers" to choose his successor. If a king displeases them, the *Ogboni* can order his suicide. Each member of the *Ogboni* administers a special section of the town or city over which the *oba* reigns.

The king has this title: Lord of the World and of Life, Owner of the Land, and Companion of the Gods. Each of these three "persons" of the king is represented in one of his three closest aides: 1. the *otun*, who serves as a priest of Shango, the god of thunder; 2. the *ona*, who judges disputes and serves as the king's spokesman at public ceremonies [see *Irù kèrè*]; and 3. the *osi*, who can impersonate the king, who regulates tolls and tributes, and who represents the king in battle. This aide dies with the king. The king's court also includes the *balogun*, who is the war chief. Each of these officials is sumptuously dressed and enjoys authority second only to that of the king.

The *oba* occupies a palace which looks quite similar to the other houses in the town or city except that it is higher, larger, and often decorated in one way or another. Also, the city marketplace can be found at its door. The palace of the Alake of Abeokuta is known for its totem-pole-like carvings on the verandah posts, and that of the Alafin of Oyo is marked by its gate posts carved as twins, symbolizing fertility. The halls through which Iyapò ran, in "It's All the Fault of Adam," would connect various parts of the compound, or cluster of rooms and buildings, into which the palace was laid out.

It is customary for subjects to prostrate themselves before the king. Men lay themselves flat on the floor on their stomachs and touch first the right cheek and then the left cheek to the floor in obeisance; women recline first on the right elbow and then on the left elbow, after first having wrapped their skirts lower down and loosened their bulky turbans, or head-ties.

The dignity of the *oba* is his first concern, and it was for this reason that his subjects were so shocked when their king ran from the fearsome dancing palm in "The Dancing Palm Tree"; his dignity had never before been so ruffled. Also, by virtue of being considered a "brother" to the king, in "It's All the Fault of Adam," Iyapò should have shown greater dignity than to run through the palace halls after a mouse, especially as underdressed as he was.

Although it is not so stated in the story "The King and the Ring," No-King-Is-as-Great-as-God would not automatically have become king after the reigning king's death (probably a suicide ordered by the *Ogboni*), but would have been chosen king by the "kingmakers" after due deliberation.

PALM TREE: The principal asset of Nigeria is the oil palm, from which are harvested palm oil and palm kernels. Palm trees of one kind or another furnish the Yorubas with roofs, walls, mats, cooking oil, coconuts, and leaves for salads, in addition to the frosty pink palm wine which is Nigeria's national drink.

PROVERBS: Proverbs, wise sayings used in folk speech, are very common in the Yorubas' storytelling as well as in their conversation. Such expressions as "That I ate and was satisfied yesterday does not serve to meet my hunger today," "The god who favors a lazy man does not exist," and "A wise man does not confide his secrets to a stranger" are very much matters of Nigerian policy of living. A man who wishes to make an especially strong point in a conversation or argument will express it in the form of a commonly accepted proverb, and he will be considered to have won the argument; this is true even in court cases.

RELIGION: Although many Yorubas have been converted to Christianity—largely to the Baptist denomination—many are still "animists"; that is, they worship the spirits of such things as thunder, war, the river, various trees, and the sea. They acknowledge one god above all: Olorun, the Owner of Heaven. In addition to Olorun, they recognize four hundred deities, with some gods and goddesses receiving primary attention among one group of Yorubas, while other gods and goddesses are honored by other groups of Yorubas. Sacrifices are offered regularly to selected deities, and their aid is implored for various undertakings. The deities' names are even incorporated into the christening names of children to give the children extra protection. Unanswered prayers are accounted for by assuming that some evil spirit interfered with the deity appealed to; to bypass such an event, sacrifice is offered first to Eshu, the devil, so that he will not be tempted to intervene in the answering of prayers. A small sampling of the deities includes the following:

> *Shango, the god of thunder and lightning*
> *Dada, the god of vegetables*
> *Ogun, the god of iron and war*
> *Shankpana, the god of smallpox*
> *Oya, the goddess of the River Niger*
> *Oke, the god of mountains*

Even among the Yorubas who have been converted to Christianity, there is a profound respect for the deities of the Yoruba pantheon, and personal tragedies or anxieties in a family may stimulate at least a temporary return to the old forms of worship.

ROBE: In "The Dancing Palm Tree" when the king draws his robe around him, he is gathering up the folds of an elaborately embroidered silk or velvet ankle-length *agbada*, a loose, flowing robe generally worn by men among the Yorubas; the back of the robe is open and rounded, and the sleeves are long and wide. With the robe he wears a matching pair of loose trousers called *sokoto*, which come just to the ankles or a little above, and which are gathered about his waist by a cord, rather than by a belt. Beneath the robe he wears first a *buba*, or blouse, with sleeves, and over it a *dansiki*, a loose, sleeveless vest that falls below the waist. On his head he wears, instead of the common *fila* (a skullcap about ten inches high, bent in upon itself at the top, and either plain or richly embroidered), a crown, two- or three-tiered and all a-glitter. And on his feet he wears handsomely worked slippers with silver or gold embroidery. Servants support above his head a tremendous, ornate umbrella to shield him from the sun. The king's clothing differs from that of his male subjects not in kind, but in elegance of material, in workmanship of the decorations, and in ornateness.

In general, men are dressed more elaborately in Yorubaland than are the women. The women wear as their basic article of clothing a wraparound skirt called the *iro*, made of a three-yard length of cloth composed of sixteen or more separate strips of cloth sewed together side by side to make one piece. This *iro* can be worn wrapped around the waist, or it may be wrapped higher up. If it is wrapped around the waist, it is used with a blouse called a *buba*, usually with long, full sleeves; if the skirt is wrapped high, a blouse may not be used at all. Around the waist are worn two sashes, the first one called the *iborun* and the one over it—a long and very wide one—called the *oja*. The *oja* is especially useful because it can be slung around the back in such a fashion as to carry a baby very conveniently and safely; it can also be used to carry articles which cannot be carried on the head. The most arresting part of a woman's clothing, however, is her ample turban, or head-tie (*gele*), made of strips of bright-colored cloth about ten yards long. If these strips are woven, it requires about seven strips side by side to make a piece wide enough for a head-tie. The *gele* is arranged afresh each time a woman goes out; when the arrangement is finished, the two ends stand out like small sails. The colors used in all her garments are gay ones, with various shades of blue the color preferred by Yoruba women—and by men, too, for that matter. Women generally go barefooted, partly because shoes are an expensive item and partly because they are uncomfortable in this hot climate.

Women's clothing, because of its simplicity, requires no special tailoring, but men's clothing, being elaborately cut and embroidered, is a matter for a trained tailor. Such craftsmen can be seen in the marketplace treadling their sewing machines between chats with customers. Clothing sales are brisk in the marketplace, and good tailors are much in demand.

TABLE: In "The Hunter and the Hind," the words *table* and *bed* and *attic* appear. The storyteller knew that tables and beds and attics did not belong in Nigerian stories, but he was trying to translate Nigerian life into terms his American listeners would understand.

Nigerian homes rarely use furniture such as beds, tables, and chairs. Instead, people sit on mats on the floor, and eat from bowls set on the floor or ground; they sleep on mats on the floor, also. Sometimes a family which is more wealthy than its neighbors will buy a chair or two to set out for visitors who might not be comfortable sitting on the floor, especially in western clothes. If they do not have chairs, the Nigerian hosts may furnish an elegant leopard skin or buffalo skin to sit on. As for the Yorubas, they are quite at ease on the floor.

The houses in which the Yorubas live are usually made of mud and wattle, with mud ceilings, and with the roofs securely thatched with a tall grass called *Bere*, so cleverly woven that not even the hardest tropical rain can make its way through. The walls are rarely more than seven or eight feet high, so there would scarcely be room or occasion for an attic. Such few valuables as the family might possess are kept in pots or bags made of bamboo fibers and placed in one corner of the sleeping room so that they can be quickly carried out in case of emergency. The hind skin in "The Hunter and the Hind" was probably hidden in just such a fashion, rather than in the "attic."

TOLL: In "It's All the Fault of Adam," when Iyapò is returning to his town after cutting wood in the forest, he has to pay the gateman a toll before he is permitted to enter. The gateman, by virtue of his need to remain always on the job, is unable to work a farm for himself, and he is thus dependent upon tolls for his living. The rate of toll is fixed by the *osi*, one of the king's aides, and it is paid usually in goods—for example, in a few sticks of the wood carried by the woodcutter, or by a yam, or by a calabash. At one time, the gateman guarded the town against surprise attacks by enemy tribes or by slave raiders, performing a most important service to the town.

Glossary

TORTOISE: In Yoruba folktales, the tortoise is considered the cleverest of the creatures. In "The Dancing Palm Tree," Tortoise finally gets his "comeuppance," but not before he has had his days of triumph. In common with other animals in Nigerian folktales, Tortoise lives as people do, and eats what they enjoy eating.

TRANSFORMATIONS: In "The Hunter and the Hind" and in "A Secret Told to a Stranger" and in "Tortoise and Babarinsa's Daughters," a change or transformation is made from one kind of living form to another. Such transformations are common in Nigerian tales, where the relationship among men and animals and even foods is unusually close and friendly. Of course, transformations are found in the folktales of other countries, also; the Grimms' "The Six Swans" is only one of many examples. In most cases, the transformation is a secret, and if the secret is ever told, unhappiness is sure to follow. All three of these Nigerian tales reveal the importance of keeping such secrets, along with the other truths they carry.

TWO WIVES: In Nigeria, except among those converted to Christianity, polygamy is a common practice. A man who intends to work a farm of any size feels that he needs more than one wife to help him. Also, since his source of income is small, he benefits by having a wife or two who enjoy going to trade in the marketplace, as indeed many wives do. In addition, a man gains status in the community according to the number of wives and children he has, a factor which increases his interest in adding as many wives as he can manage. Ordinarily, the first wife enjoys a special position in the household; if she remains childless, however, she may find herself bypassed for a newer wife.

Each of the wives, with her young children, occupies a separate room or small building in the compound, or group of houses, within the same mud wall. The open space at the center of the compound is used for cooking space by all the wives, as well as for tethering such animals as they may own within the family. Several related families often share the same compound, and this living group may even include close friends and their families. The Yorubas are very sociable, and enjoy the close groupings afforded by a compound arrangement.

Interestingly, within the compound any mother who wishes can punish any child who is misbehaving—at the risk, of course, of annoying the child's own mother. In practice, children are spanked very little, and they learn early to be helpful within their own small community, so they have little time to be naughty.

WINDING STREETS: In "The King and the Ring," the woman hurries home through "the winding streets." The streets of Yoruba villages and towns and cities are not laid out in orderly fashion, in parallel lines, to make it possible to find one's way easily; they are instead constructed almost as mazes, with no plan at all except, seemingly, to confuse. And that was precisely the purpose for their winding: to slow down and confuse the members of enemy tribes who might enter the town to do battle or to plunder or, worse, to seek slaves. In addition to laying out their streets in deliberately haphazard fashion, the Yorubas constructed thick, strong mud walls around their towns.